Five reasons why you'll love Isadora Moon...

Meet the magical,
fang-tastic Isadora Moon!

Isadora's cuddly toy, Pink Rabbit,
has been magicked to life!

Get ready for some
magical mischief!

Isadora's family is crazy!

Enchanting
pink and black
pictures

What would you do if you were shrunk down to tiny size for a day?

I would look for fairies in the garden
and play hide and seek!
– Ava

I'd play in my doll house.
– Thea

I would probably make friends
with the rats and mice.
– Noah

I would have a warm bath in
someone's cup of coffee!
– Georgia

I would make a spider friend.
– Joshan

I would sneak my costume on and
dive into my fish tank!
– Bella

I'd make friends with a cute mouse.
– Bobby

Family Tree

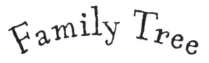

My Mum
Countess Cordelia
Moon

Baby Honeyblossom

My Dad
Count Bartholomew
Moon

Me!
Isadora Moon

Pink Rabbit

For vampires, fairies and humans everywhere!
And for my own little Honeyblossom, Celestine Stardust.

OXFORD
UNIVERSITY PRESS

Great Clarendon Street, Oxford OX2 6DP
Oxford University Press is a department of the University of Oxford.
It furthers the University's objective of excellence in research, scholarship,
and education by publishing worldwide. Oxford is a registered trade mark
of Oxford University Press in the UK and in certain other countries

Text copyright © Harriet Muncaster 2021
Illustration copyright © Harriet Muncaster 2021

The moral rights of the author have been asserted

Database right Oxford University Press (maker)

First published in 2021

British Library Cataloguing in Publication Data

Data available

ISBN:978-0-19-277953-3

3 5 7 9 10 8 6 4

Printed in Great Britain by Bell and Bain Ltd, Glasgow

Paper used in the production of this book is a natural,
recyclable product made from wood grown in sustainable forests.
The manufacturing process conforms to the environmental
regulations of the country of origin.

MIX
Paper from
responsible sources
FSC® C007785
www.fsc.org

ISADORA MOON

Goes to a Wedding

Harriet Muncaster

OXFORD
UNIVERSITY PRESS

Chapter ONE

'Aunt Crystal is getting married!'
exclaimed Mum one frosty and sparkling
winter morning. She held up the
snowflake-shaped invitation so that we
could all see.

'Isadora, you're going to be a
bridesmaid! Along with Honeyblossom
and your cousin Mirabelle.'

'A bridesmaid!' I shouted, jumping up from my chair and accidentally dropping my toast onto the floor. 'I've never been a bridesmaid before!' I began to leap and dance around the room with Pink Rabbit bouncing along behind me.

Pink Rabbit used to be my favourite cuddly toy but my mum magicked him alive with her wand. She can do things like that because she's a fairy.

'I expect you'll have to wear something really beautiful,' said Mum as she continued reading the invitation. 'Aunt Crystal is marrying a summer fairy. He's called Wren. It's going to be a frosty and flowery wedding!'

'Brr!' said Dad, wrapping his vampire cape more tightly around him. 'I will have to wear my woollen vest. I'm sure there will be lots of snow fairies there like Aunt Crystal. They always make the room so cold!'

A few days later there was a knock on the door and a big package arrived at our house.

'I wonder what it is,' said Mum as she carried it through to the kitchen where my baby sister Honeyblossom was sitting in her high chair. 'It looks important.' She got some scissors and began to cut it open and I watched as clouds of icy silver glitter puffed up into the air.

'Ooh!' said Mum as she pulled out two beautiful pale pink dresses, sparkling all over with snowflakes, flowers, and fairy frost. 'These must be for the wedding!'

'Wow,' I breathed. 'Can I try mine on?'

'I think you'd better!' said Mum, handing me my dress. The skirt rustled as I stepped into it, and tiny little snowflakes twinkled icily up at me. It felt very special.

'Oh Isadora!' gasped Mum. 'You look magical! It's a shame Dad's not down here to see it.'

My dad is a vampire and he sleeps through the day, getting up in the evening for 'breakfast'. We always have two breakfasts in our house.

'I'll just keep it on until Dad wakes up,' I said hopefully but Mum shook her head.

'Absolutely not,' she said. 'We need to keep it in perfect condition for the wedding day.' She rummaged in the package again and pulled out two flower crowns and

a jar of something glittery.
'Wing dust!' said
Mum. 'It will make your
little bat wings sparkly. And
look at these!' She handed me one of the
flower crowns and put the other one on
Honeyblossom who immediately tried to
pull it off with her chubby little hands. I
stared in awe at the flower
crown. It had been
frosted all over with
an icy fairy spell and
each petal shimmered
and glittered in the
afternoon light.

Carefully I lowered it onto my head.

'Just beautiful!' sighed Mum, gazing at Honeyblossom and me. 'You two are going to be the most wonderful vampire fairy bridesmaids that anyone's ever seen!'

Chapter TWO

On the morning of the wedding I woke up early, too excited to sleep. It was still dark outside but I could just make out the outline of my bridesmaid's dress hanging up at the end of my bed, glimmering in the moonlight.

'Oh Pink Rabbit!' I whispered, hugging him tight. 'I can't wait!'

Pink Rabbit snuggled into me, still
sleepy, so I wrapped him up in my duvet
and got out of bed, hoping that the rest
of my family would
be up soon.

The house was quiet as I padded around
it. Even Dad had gone to sleep at a
reasonable hour seeing as he would have
to stay awake for the wedding. I didn't
know what to do with myself. I was too
excited to sleep, but waiting for everyone

else to get up was very boring. In the end
I went up to the attic and had a chat with
my friend Oscar the ghost.

'Why don't you make breakfast for
everyone?' he suggested. 'I'll help.'

'That's a great idea!' I said, wishing

that I had thought of it myself. We flew down to the kitchen together and I set the table while Oscar made bat-shaped pancakes on the stove. He's allowed to use the stove by himself because he's more than two hundred years old!

'Something smells delicious!' said Mum as she came into the kitchen half an hour later.

'We made pancakes!' I said, pulling out Mum's chair so that she could sit down, and then draping a napkin over her lap. 'This one's yours, with all the fresh fruit on it. Look—I gave it blueberry eyes!'

'Lovely!' smiled Mum and began to eat. Dad came in a little while later, wearing his sunglasses and yawning.

'Too early,' he complained as he sat

down at the table. But he immediately perked up when he saw the breakfast that I had made him. Oscar had helped me to put red food colouring in the batter and then we had covered the finished pancakes all over with raspberry jam. Vampires only like red food.

'Scrumptious!' exclaimed Dad as he tucked in. 'This will keep me going during the wedding!'

It seemed to take forever to get ready that morning. Dad spent a long time choosing which woollen cape he was going to wear and smoothing his hair down with extra strong shiny vampire gel. Mum carefully put on a delicate pink dress made of real rose petals that smelt like perfume, and Honeyblossom and I had to wait until they were both ready before we could put on our bridesmaid's dresses.

'You don't want to ruin them before

the wedding's even started!' said Mum as she helped me to fix the flower crown into my hair at last and sprinkled my bat wings all over with the sparkling wing dust from the jar. I ran over to the mirror and did a twirl.

Everything shimmered and twinkled. I had never felt so magical!

'Enchanting!' said Dad when he saw Honeyblossom and me. Then we all went downstairs to wait by the front door.

'The fairy sledge should be here soon!' said Mum, peering out of the window.

'A fairy sledge?' I said. 'Aren't we going in the car?'

Mum looked at me and laughed.

'All the way to the winter fairy realm?' she said. 'I don't think so! Aunt Crystal has sent out magic fairy sledges for all the guests. I must have forgotten to tell you!'

I hopped up and down with excitement. A magic

fairy sledge! It was

the best surprise!

I pressed my nose

to the window

as rain drizzled

down outside

and watched and

waited. Eventually

a big, glittering carriage, carved from ice
and decorated all over with pink and white
flowers, drew up outside our front gate.
Dad put up his umbrella and we all
hurried out towards it. I sat down on one

of the velvet-cushioned seats and Mum
sat down next to me, holding tightly onto
Honeyblossom.

The carriage jerked into life and I
craned my neck out of the window as the

sledge began to whizz along the road on its icy runners, lifting up into the air and starting to soar across the sky. It went very fast and it wasn't long before the drops of rain outside turned into big fluffy snowflakes and the ground below became a carpet of white.

'We must be almost there!' said Mum and she wrapped her coat around her more tightly. Mum is a summer fairy and she feels the cold.

Eventually I spotted something glistening in the distance. It was a huge, beautiful building with icy turrets that pointed up towards the sky and sparkled like glass in the sunshine.

'It's the Ice Hall,' said Mum. 'That's where we're going. It's fairy tradition for the bride to choose the place where she gets married. I knew Aunt Crystal would want something wintery!'

Our sledge swooshed through the air and then landed with a crunch on the snow by the entrance. There were other fairy sledges landing nearby too, and as I jumped down from ours I spotted my cousins and my Aunt Seraphina and Uncle Alvin.

'Look!' I said. 'It's Mirabelle and Wilbur!'

I started to run across the snow towards them. It's always exciting to see Mirabelle, even though she does get me into trouble sometimes. She was wearing the same bridesmaid's dress as me and also a pair of fairy wings that glittered with frosty sparkles.

'Aunt Crystal sent them to me with the dress,' said Mirabelle. 'Just to wear for the wedding. They're enchanted ones. Look, I can fly!' She flapped up into the air to show me. Mirabelle is half witch,

half fairy but she wasn't born with any wings.

'Aunt Crystal sent some to Wilbur too,' said Mirabelle. 'But he's refusing to wear them.'

'Wizards don't have fairy wings,' said Wilbur firmly.

We all made our way towards the entrance of the Ice Hall, which had been beautifully decorated with an arbour of perfumed summer flowers. Inside it was very crowded with lots of fairies milling about in their smartest suits and most glamorous dresses.

'There's Granny and Grandpa!' said Mirabelle, pointing. We ran over and gave them each a big hug before Mum pulled us away and said it was time to go and find Aunt Crystal. She led us to a private room and we slipped inside.

'Aunt Crystal!' I gasped. She looked spellbinding! She was wearing a long dress made completely from snowflakes and frosted white petals and in her hair was a wreath of flowers just like mine. She glittered and dazzled all over.

'Just in time!' smiled Aunt Crystal. 'Cordelia, will you help me with my veil?'

'Of course!' said Mum and handed Honeyblossom to me to look after.

We had to wait quite a long time in the little room while Aunt Crystal finished getting ready, and the fairies outside in the great hall all started to take their seats. I began to feel a little nervous at the thought of having to walk down the aisle in front of everyone but Mirabelle squeezed my hand.

'It will be fine!' she whispered. 'Just pretend you're doing one of your ballet shows!'

At last Aunt Crystal was ready and I heard the chattering outside die down. Mum handed Wilbur, Mirabelle, and me a basket of pink flower petals each. Then a fairy poked his head round the door and said, 'It's time!'

Chapter THREE

There was a huge gasp from the wedding
guests as Aunt Crystal walked out into
the hall and everyone turned to look at
her. She began to glide slowly down the
aisle to some beautiful tinkly fairy music.
Mirabelle, Wilbur, and I followed her
proudly, scattering flower petals on the
ground from our baskets, like we had been

told to. There was a tall summer fairy
in a pink and white striped suit waiting
for Aunt Crystal at the end of the aisle.
He took her hand and smiled. They both
looked so happy.

'If I ever get married,' whispered Mirabelle as we took our seats at the front of the great hall, 'I'm going to have a silver dress made of spiderwebs!'

★ ★ ★

The ceremony started and Mirabelle, Wilbur, and I tried our best not to fidget or whisper to each other. But it was hard. There was so much talking and singing. It just went on and on! At last there was a loud chiming of bells, everyone cheered, and Aunt Crystal walked back up the aisle holding the hand of her new husband, Wren. All around us fairies threw confetti until a blizzard of petals and snowflakes swirled throughout the great hall.

'Thank goodness that's over!' said Mirabelle. 'That was boring, wasn't it!'

'Mmm,' I said, not wanting to be rude about Aunt Crystal's wedding even though I had found it quite boring too.

We found our parents and then followed them into a banqueting hall and towards a round table with a huge flowery centrepiece in the middle of it. I sat down next to Mirabelle with Honeyblossom on the other side of me in her high chair. She was a bit grizzly after having sat through the whole ceremony.

'This looks yummy!' said Mirabelle as waiters started to come round the room with plates of fairy food on silver platters. We gobbled our lunch down and then waited for pudding. There were lots of delicious-looking desserts on a table on the other side of the room. I could see a big creamy trifle and a fluffy meringue pie and a bowl of fairy fruit salad.

'I'm going to have a big bit of everything!' said Mirabelle greedily.

'Me too!' I said.

But it turned out that we couldn't have pudding straight away. We had to listen to the speeches first. Grandpa got up and talked for a long time and then Aunt

Crystal's new husband, Wren, did a speech.

Wilbur started filling in his *Wizard's Book of Word Searches* under the table, and Mirabelle and I sank further and further down in our seats from boredom. We hadn't brought anything to do! Pink Rabbit yawned and fell asleep under my chair.

'Why don't you two go out into the entrance hall and play for a bit,' Mum whispered. 'Aunt Crystal won't mind. You can take Honeyblossom with you. She's very restless.'

Mirabelle and I looked at each other. That sounded like a great plan! Mum carefully put Honeyblossom in my arms and I did my best to carry her out. She was quite heavy and I was glad to put her down on the floor once we were back in the entrance hall. She started crawling around, delighted to be free.

She flapped her little wings and bobbed up and down in the air. Honeyblossom can't walk yet but she is just learning to use her wings.

'Wow!' I said as I stared around us. The entrance hall looked different from when we had first come into it. There was a big table in the corner, heaving with shiny presents wrapped up in ribbons, and in the middle of the floor was another, smaller table that had something very magical on it. Something that hadn't been there before.

'The wedding cake!' gasped Mirabelle.

We both ran over and gazed up at the delectable creation. It was the most beautiful cake I had ever seen and shaped like a fairy castle. Little silver balls glinted out from swirls of piped buttercream, and flowery turrets reached up into the air, topped off with pointed roofs of spun sugar. I looked at Mirabelle and noticed that her eyes had gone very dark and glinty, just like they do when she is about to cause mischief.

'Isadora,' she said after a moment,
'do you remember the time we shrank
ourselves and went and played inside your
doll's house? It was fun, wasn't it?'

'Yes,' I agreed.

'Well, I've got an idea,' said
Mirabelle. 'Why don't we shrink ourselves
again? I've brought some of my
witchy magic with me. We
could go into the cake and
eat as much of it as we
want to! We'd be so tiny
we could eat until we
burst!'

'No way!' I said,
shaking my head fiercely.

Last time I had let Mirabelle drag me into one of her mischievous plans we had both got into a lot of trouble.

'Oh, come on!' begged Mirabelle. 'It would be so much fun! Aunt Crystal will never know!'

'No,' I said again. I was determined to stand up for myself this time. 'It would be unfair on Aunt Crystal. It's her special wedding cake!'

'Oh, OK,' shrugged Mirabelle. She turned away and I ran across the room to get Honeyblossom who had fluttered over to the present table and was starting to play with the ribbons. I carried her back over to the cake.

'Look!' I pointed. 'Pretty!'

Mirabelle reached into the folds of her bridesmaid skirt and from a hidden pocket pulled out a little compact mirror with a powder puff in it.

'Why have you got that?' I asked, starting to feel worried. The pink powder looked familiar. Very much like the potion we had used to shrink ourselves last time.

Mirabelle didn't reply. She was too busy dipping the little puff into the glittering powder and dabbing it onto her cheeks. Honeyblossom wriggled in my arms. She stretched out her chubby hands and tried to grab the powder puff.

'No Honeyblossom!' I said, stepping back. But it was too late. Honeyblossom had already grabbed the puff and was starting to stroke it across her cheeks.

'Bunny tail!' she smiled. 'Soft!'

'Give it back, Honeyblossom,' I said and hurriedly pulled the little puff out of her hands, getting powder all over my fingers.

'Don't touch it, Isadora!' said
Mirabelle and snatched the puff back,
putting it back inside the compact mirror
and closing it with a click. She stared at
me in dismay and her face went very red.

'I was just going to use it on myself!'
she said.

Suddenly there was a

POOF!

of pink smoke and my tummy lurched as though it was being pulled downwards. I watched in horror as we all began to shrink, becoming smaller and smaller until we were the size of tiny dolls. The table with the cake on it towered above us.

Chapter FOUR

'MIRABELLE!' I shouted angrily.

'It's not my fault!' cried Mirabelle.
'You weren't supposed to touch it!'

'Turn us back to the right size
straightaway!' I demanded and reached
out for Honeyblossom who was fluttering
up into the air, as light as a feather. Then
I had a horrible thought.

'Is this exactly the same as the last potion we used to shrink ourselves?' I asked. 'That took twenty whole minutes to wear off!'

'No,' said Mirabelle. 'This is a different one we've been learning to make at witch school. You only have to puff a bit more of the powder onto your skin and you'll grow to your full size again. It's foolproof! Don't worry!'

'Oh good,' I said, feeling relieved. 'Give me the compact then! Now!'

But Mirabelle flapped into the air with her special bridesmaid's

fairy wings and disappeared into the cake.

'I'll give it to you in a minute,' she called. 'I promise! But come up here and look at the cake first. It's so beautiful!'

'Don't touch anything Mirabelle!' I shouted and rose up into the air towards the cake with Honeyblossom, landing gently on a whirl of ivory-coloured buttercream. Honeyblossom wriggled to be free so I put her down carefully on top of a pink sugar flower.

Mirabelle was right. The cake was beautiful, like a magical wonderland! For a moment I forgot to be cross with my cousin. It was mesmerizing to be surrounded by icing flowers and sugar snowflakes. Everything smelt sweet and delicious. I couldn't help touching one of the walls of the fairy castle with my finger and poking out just the tiniest, tiniest bit of buttercream. It tasted amazing. I scooped out a teeny bit more. Aunt Crystal really

would never notice; we were so small!

'See, I told you this was a fun idea!' said Mirabelle.

Now I had started eating the cake it was hard to stop! I kept poking my finger into the walls and eating just a little bit more and then a little bit more. I tried to be careful, smoothing the icing back down with my hand so that there were no marks in it, but it definitely didn't look quite as neat as before. I felt a flicker of panic and glanced over at my cousin.

'Mirabelle!' I gasped.

She was down on her hands and knees, surrounded by a pattern of sticky footprints and she had stuck her arm so far down into the buttercream that it had completely disappeared. She was scooping out great handfuls of the cake and stuffing

it into her mouth, as fast as she could.
There was icing everywhere—round her
mouth and on her dress and in her hair.

Suddenly I felt horrified at what we
were doing.

'Mirabelle!' I said. 'We have to stop!'

Mirabelle looked up at me but she
kept eating the cake.

'You'll make yourself sick!' I said. 'Aunt Crystal's definitely going to notice all these holes!'

Mirabelle stared around her at the footprints and mess she had made of the icing and a guilty expression flashed across her face. She stopped chewing and started to look a bit worried.

'Maybe I got a bit carried away,' she admitted. 'You can fix it though, can't you Isadora? With your wand!'

'My wand's back at the table in the banqueting hall,' I said, starting to feel furious with Mirabelle all over again. 'What about *your* witch magic?'

'I only have the powder puff,' said

Mirabelle, looking a little sheepish. 'That's not going to be much help.' She stood up and waded through the icing towards me.

'I'm sorry Isadora,' she said. 'I didn't think it through properly.'

'You never think it through!' I said.

'Well, you didn't *have* to eat the cake,' said Mirabelle and I felt myself blush. She was right about that.

'Listen,' said Mirabelle. 'Let's not argue. I've got an idea. Let's make ourselves big again. Then we can go back to the table in the banqueting hall and get your wand to fix the cake!'

'OK,' I agreed. It wasn't a bad idea and I couldn't think of a better solution. I looked around me for Honeyblossom so that we could make her big too and then

froze. Where was she? Now that I thought about it I hadn't seen her for a few minutes. I had been too distracted by Mirabelle.

'Where's Honeyblossom?' I said. 'She's gone!'

'She can't have gone,' said Mirabelle. 'She was here a moment ago.'

'I forgot to watch her!' I said, my voice coming out all high-pitched with panic. 'I can't see her anywhere!'

I flew up into the air until I was high above the cake and searched wildly all around the entrance hall. I couldn't see her by the present table or among the flowers or anywhere near the cake. Where was my baby sister? She would be even harder to find now that she was tiny!

'We have to go and tell Mum and Dad!' I wailed.

'No!' said Mirabelle quickly. 'We can't do that! They'll find out what we've done!'

'I don't care!' I said. 'It's more important that we find her!'

I started to fly across the room towards the open door of the banqueting hall. I didn't even care that I was still doll-sized. I was going to find Mum and Dad.

'Wait!' shouted Mirabelle from behind me. 'We can't tell them! They'll be so cross!'

'I don't care!' I shouted again. 'Honeyblossom might be in danger!'

'She won't be in danger!' said Mirabelle. 'She can't have gone far. She's probably just flown into the banqueting hall.

Let's go and look for her ourselves before we tell anyone. We don't want to make a scene at Aunt Crystal's wedding!'

I slowed down. Mirabelle had a point. We definitely didn't want to ruin Aunt Crystal's wedding if there was a chance we could find Honeyblossom ourselves.

'OK, fine!' I said. 'But if we don't find her in ten minutes then we have to tell Mum and Dad.'

We flew into the banqueting hall together. All the guests  were still sitting at their tables and the speeches were still droning on. I noticed

that some fairies had
actually fallen asleep!
Wilbur was still busy
filling in his *Wizard's
Book of Word Searches.*

Mirabelle flew up high in the air
making sure that we stayed up by the
ceiling where no one was likely to spot
us. We flew in and out of the tinkling
chandeliers and round and round the
room, looking everywhere for a sign of
my baby sister. But she was nowhere to be
seen.

'It's no use,' I said after about ten
minutes. 'We're never going to spot her
in here. She's too tiny! We really need to

let Mum and Dad know. What if someone steps on her?'

Mirabelle's face went very white at the thought.

'OK,' she agreed. 'Let's tell them.'

I flapped my wings and started to make my way across the room towards where Mum and Dad were sitting. But then something made me stop. It was a small movement on the pudding table down below. My heart leapt as I realized who it was.

'Look!' I whispered.

Floating inside a ring of sliced pineapple in the fruit salad bowl was Honeyblossom! She looked very happy.

'We found her!' I said. 'Let's go and get her out. We'll have to do it without anyone noticing!'

We started to fly slowly down towards the bowl of fruit salad, hoping that no one would look in our direction.

We were almost there when suddenly the room erupted with applause and everyone started to get up out of their seats and make their way towards the pudding table. Towards us! I stared at Mirabelle in dismay. There was no way we would be able to rescue Honeyblossom without anyone noticing now!

Unless . . .

'Mirabelle!' I hissed. 'Follow me!'

I flapped my wings as hard as I could and flew underneath the table just as the first guests came up to get their pudding.

'We need to get big again!' I said. 'Quickly! Then we can scoop her out with the spoon ourselves! It will just look like we've come to get our pudding.'

'OK!' said Mirabelle. Hurriedly
she rummaged in her skirt for the
compact and handed it to me. I
dabbed some of the powder onto
my hands with the puff, making
sure to stay hunched in a ball under
the table. I didn't want to bang
my head when I grew big! There
was a puff of pink smoke and then
another one from Mirabelle and
we were both the right size again.

I lifted up a corner of the tablecloth and crawled out, hoping that no one would notice.

'What are you two doing down there?' said a familiar voice and Mirabelle and I stood up quickly. It was Grandpa!

'I know what you're up to,' he said and I felt my cheeks go red. 'You're trying to jump the pudding queue!'

'Oh!' I said 'Umm . . .'

'It's all right,' chuckled Grandpa, 'You can slip in after me. I expect you're hungry after sitting through all those speeches!'

'We are!' said Mirabelle but I saw her go a bit green at the mention of pudding. Her eyes were on the fruit salad where Honeyblossom was still floating around happily in the slice of pineapple. Her wings would surely be all wet with fruit juice and I knew she wouldn't be able to fly. We had to rescue her quickly!

Grandpa bent down and started to peer

closely at all the puddings. I felt my heart begin to pitter-patter in my chest. Would he spot Honeyblossom? But Grandpa is quite shortsighted and he wasn't wearing his glasses. He didn't seem to notice her.

'The fruit salad looks healthy, doesn't it?' he said and picked up the serving spoon. Feeling desperate, I shot out my hand to pluck Honeyblossom out of the bowl, but Grandpa got there first! He scooped up my sister and plopped her into his pudding bowl along with the ring of sliced pineapple and some other pieces of fruit.

'Isadora!' said Grandpa, surprised. 'You're supposed to use a spoon for the fruit salad, not your hands! It's polite to

wait your turn!' He handed me the spoon
and I stood there in shock as he walked off
with Honeyblossom in his pudding bowl.
Mirabelle stared at me, aghast.

'What are we going to do now?' she
asked. 'What if Grandpa *eats* her?'

'Oh no! I didn't think of that!' I said,
quickly putting the spoon
back into the fruit salad
and turning away from
the pudding table. 'We
have to rescue her!
You'll have to distract
him while I pick her out
of his bowl.'

'OK,' nodded Mirabelle. 'That sounds like a good plan.'

We pushed through the crowd of fairies all queuing up for their pudding and hurried over to the top table where Grandpa was sitting right next to his daughter, Aunt Crystal. Luckily Aunt Crystal had her back turned towards him—she was busy smiling at Wren!

Mirabelle and I sidled up to the table next to Grandpa.

'Hello again,' he said. 'I thought you two were getting your pudding?'

'We're going to in a minute,' said Mirabelle. 'I just wanted to tell you something important first!'

'Oh?' said Grandpa and dipped his spoon into his bowl, scooping up Honeyblossom. I held my breath and moved closer to him, hoping to be able to snatch her while he was distracted.

'I . . . I won a prize at witch school last week!' said Mirabelle loudly.

'It was for . . . um . . . being the best
potion-maker in the class!'

'Marvellous!' said Grandpa. He
looked impressed. But he was still moving
his spoon closer and closer towards his
mouth. I stared desperately at Mirabelle
and she stared desperately back at me.

'Grandpa!' I shouted
and pulled on his arm
just as he opened
his mouth to pop
Honeyblossom into it.
She fell off the spoon
and slid down his beard
into his top pocket.

'What is it, Isadora?' said Grandpa,

starting to sound a little annoyed. 'Look, you've made me spill my fruit salad!' He reached into his top pocket and whipped out a handkerchief to dab up the fruit juice.

Mirabelle and I watched in horror as Honeyblossom came flying out. She whizzed through the air and landed on Aunt Crystal's lap with a damp plop. Aunt Crystal jumped in surprise and looked down.

'Honeyblossom?' she gasped.

Chapter FIVE

'Oh no,' I whispered.

Aunt Crystal picked up my little sister and put her on her hand.

'What on earth has happened to you?' she said, holding Honeyblossom up close to her face. 'You're tiny!'

Grandpa leaned over to peer
at Aunt Crystal's hand. Then he
turned and looked disapprovingly
at Mirabelle and me. I felt like I
was shrinking all over again. But
Aunt Crystal didn't seem too upset.

'Let's not worry about it!'
she said. 'This day is too happy to
spoil.' She picked up her powerful
snowflake wand from the table and
waved it over Honeyblossom.

Icy glitter and snowy stars sparkled in the air for a moment and Honeyblossom appeared full size again, looking damp, sticky, and confused, on Aunt Crystal's lap.

'I'll take her!' I said, holding out my arms to Aunt Crystal. 'I think she needs a change!' But Aunt Crystal shook her head.

'I think Honeyblossom needs to go back to your mum and dad,' she said. 'Where are they? Cordelia! Bartholomew!'

Mum and Dad came hurrying over.

'There you are!' said Dad when he saw Mirabelle and me. 'We were worried for a moment. You weren't in the entrance hall when we looked. It's pudding time!'

'Why is Honeyblossom all damp and sticky?' asked Mum as she took my sister from Aunt Crystal and gave her a hug. 'And why is Mirabelle covered in . . . icing?'

'Umm,' said Mirabelle as Mum and Dad ushered us away from the top table and back to our own table where Wilbur, Aunt Seraphina, and Uncle Alvin were sitting.

They all had bowls full of creamy trifle
and fluffy meringue pie in front of them,
and Mirabelle turned green when she saw
them.

'What's happened to you?' asked
Uncle Alvin when he saw Mirabelle's
icing-covered dress and hair.

'You've been up to mischief again, haven't you!' said Aunt Seraphina. 'What have you done this time?'

Mirabelle looked at me and I looked back at her. Neither of us dared to say anything. Aunt Seraphina is a witch and can be really scary when she's cross. But after a few moments of silence Mirabelle suddenly burst out, 'It's all my fault! I wanted to shrink so we could look around the cake and eat some of it but Honeyblossom and Isadora touched the potion by mistake too and we all shrank together! Then Honeyblossom got lost and we had to find her . . .' Her voice trailed off. Then she added, 'Isadora didn't really do anything. She was trying to get Honeyblossom back.'

'I did eat some of the cake,' I admitted. Aunt Seraphina looked furious and I was glad that she wasn't my mum. Her eyes had gone all dark and glinty.

'I can't believe you touched the wedding cake!' said Mum, sounding disappointed. 'Didn't you think about how Aunt Crystal might feel to have her cake ruined on her special day?'

'No,' said Mirabelle honestly. 'I was just too excited.'

Uncle Alvin frowned. 'You need to think a bit more about how your actions affect other people!' he said.

Mirabelle nodded but she looked a bit strange. Her face was still a pale shade of green.

'I think I'm going to be sick!' she said and ran from the room. Aunt Seraphina raised an arched eyebrow while Uncle Alvin sighed and shook his head despairingly.

'I think she might be learning her lesson,' he said.

Mum handed Honeyblossom to Dad and picked her wand up from the table.

'I think I need to go and look at this cake before it's too late,' she said. I followed her out into the entrance hall.

It was strange to look at the cake from my normal height again after having been small enough to walk on top of it. I peered in and could see tiny footprints all over the icing and a messy hole where Mirabelle had dug down into the sponge.

'Gosh,' said Mum. 'She must have eaten a lot for such a tiny person.' She waved her wand over the cake and all

the footprints and holes immediately
disappeared.

'It was very wrong
of you and Mirabelle to
touch Aunt Crystal's special wedding
cake,' said Mum. 'And very dangerous
too! Poor Honeyblossom could have been
stepped on! Or eaten!'

'I know,' I said, hanging my head. 'I'm
sorry.'

'I'm going to confiscate your wand
for a week,' said Mum. 'And you can buy
Honeyblossom something special to say
sorry with your pocket money.'

'OK,' I said in a small voice.

'And we won't mention any of this to
Aunt Crystal,' said Mum. 'There's no need
to ruin her special day.'

I breathed a sigh of relief.

Just then two fairy waiters came into the room. They had come to collect the cake and take it into the banqueting hall.

'Marvellous creation, isn't it?' said one.

'The icing is so smooth and snowy,' said the other.

The two waiters lifted up the cake into the air and carried it towards the banqueting hall. We followed them, hurrying back to our table.

There was a hush all around the room as the cake was put down in front of Aunt Crystal and her new summer fairy husband, Wren. Aunt Crystal's eyes went big and round with delight.

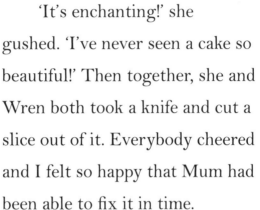

'It's enchanting!' she gushed. 'I've never seen a cake so beautiful!' Then together, she and Wren both took a knife and cut a slice out of it. Everybody cheered and I felt so happy that Mum had been able to fix it in time.

After that more waiters came into the room and cleared away all the empty cups and plates. Some music started to play and lots of fairies moved towards the

dance floor.

I looked around for
Mirabelle and saw that she had
slunk back into the room but
she didn't look well. She was
sitting on a chair along the back
wall and clutching her tummy.
I couldn't help feeling sorry for
her, especially as she had owned
up to everything being her fault.
I hurried over and sat down
beside her.

'Are you OK?' I asked. But Mirabelle just shook her head. She still looked very sick. I lifted Pink Rabbit onto her lap. 'I'm sure he won't mind keeping you company,' I said. I know that Mirabelle loves Pink Rabbit. She's always saying she wants a special pet of her own. Mirabelle put out

her hand to stroke Pink Rabbit's head but he shook it crossly and jumped back down onto the floor. He's always been suspicious of Mirabelle ever since she turned him into a miniature rabbit for two days.

'Oh, I think he wants to dance,' I said, so as not to hurt her feelings.

Mirabelle nodded, still unable to speak, and then I felt an icy breeze blow all around us and Aunt Crystal appeared.

'Hello my beautiful bridesmaids,' she said. 'Are you enjoying the wedding?'

'Oh yes!' I said. 'I loved walking down the aisle!'

'Me too,' said Mirabelle weakly. 'But I'm afraid I'm not feeling at all well now.'

'Oh dear!' said Aunt Crystal. 'What a shame! I'll have to send you home with an extra large slice of cake to make up for it!'

Mirabelle

looked horrified and her face turned green all over again.

'I have to go to the bathroom!' she said and jumped off the chair, disappearing in the direction of the toilets.

'Poor Mirabelle,' said Aunt Crystal. 'I do hope she feels better soon!'

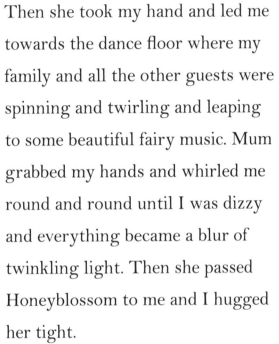

Then she took my hand and led me towards the dance floor where my family and all the other guests were spinning and twirling and leaping to some beautiful fairy music. Mum grabbed my hands and whirled me round and round until I was dizzy and everything became a blur of twinkling light. Then she passed Honeyblossom to me and I hugged her tight.

'I'm sorry Honeyblossom!'

I shouted over the music. 'I'll
never let Mirabelle use any of her
witchy potions on you ever again!'
Honeyblossom just laughed and blew
a raspberry back at me.

Outside the sky began to darken
and the stars shone out brighter than
usual.

'They must be shining for
Aunt Crystal!' I told my baby sister.
'They're shining for Aunt Crystal's
wedding day!'

Turn the page
for some
Isadorable
things to make
and do!

How to make wedding flower crowns

In the story Isadora, Honeyblossom, and Mirabelle wear beautiful flower crowns to go with their bridesmaid dresses.

Why not try to make one for yourself?

Things to collect:

★ A long piece of vine wire or twine

★ Scissors

★ Flower tape (it sticks to the flowers better than sticky tape)

★ Daisies and other small flowers (cut with permission from a grown-up!)

★ Greenery like ivy or ferns

★ A grown-up to help

Method:

1. Shape the vine wire to the size of your head. Ask a grown-up to cut it just a bit longer than you need, for a bit of wriggle room. Fix it at the right size with floral tape.

2. Wrap some of the greenery around the wire crown. Use the floral tape to hold it in place

3. Group 2-3 little flowers together into small bunches and hold together with floral tape. Make a few little bunches to spread around your crown.

4. Feed each little bunch through the greenery and vine and stick with floral tape.

5. Try it on and decide if you have enough flowers to get the look you want!

6. Keep it in the fridge to keep it fresh until you need to wear it!

Alternative option:
If you'd like your head garland to last a bit longer, you could use different-coloured tissue paper instead of fresh flowers and greenery!

How to make a confetti cone

Once you have made your confetti you
need something for it to go in!

These confetti cones are perfect.

What you will need:

★ Colourful wrapping paper

★ Scissors

★ Sticky tape

Method:

1. Cut your wrapping paper into squares.
   The bigger the square, the bigger the cone,
   but around 20cm is a good size.

2. Roll the paper up to create a cone. Make sure
   you roll it more tightly at one end, so that it
   doesn't leave a hole. You don't want your
   confetti to fall out!

3. Secure the ends of the paper with sticky tape.

4. Put your confetti in!

How to make pancakes

Weddings can be long days, so you want to make sure you have a good breakfast before you set off. Why not have pancakes just like Isadora makes for her family, with the help of Oscar the ghost?

Ingredients:

- 220g self-raising flour
- Pinch of salt
- 50g caster sugar
- 2 eggs
- 280ml milk
- 1 tbsp oil

Equipment:

- Mixing bowl
- Small bowl
- Weighing scales
- Whisk

- Frying pan
- Ladle
- Spatula
- A grown-up assistant to help

Method:

1. Add the flour, salt, and sugar to the mixing bowl.

2. Beat egg and milk together in the small bowl.

3. Slowly add the egg and milk to the mixing bowl while you whisk.

4. Heat the frying pan to medium and add a little oil.

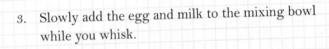

5. When the pan is hot, add a small amount of batter (around 2 tablespoons) to the pan. Depending on the size of your pan you can do about three at a time.

6. When bubbles start to pop on the top it is time to flip your pancakes with the spatula!

7. After about a minute check if they are golden brown, and if so remove them from the heat.

8. Enjoy with a topping of your choice!

If your batter is thick enough you can try and make shapes with it when you pour it into the pan, such as bats! It makes it easier to do this if you make slightly larger pancakes.

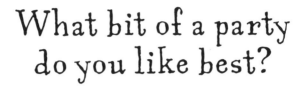

What bit of a party do you like best?

Take the quiz to find out!

If you hear music playing, what do you do?

A. Look around, and see if you can see anyone nodding to the beat.

B. Hope it might be the ice cream man.

C. Get up and start dancing, of course!

What do you like to do in your spare time?

A. People watching.

B. Baking.

C. Making up dance routines.

Where is your favourite room in your house?

A. The living room, where the family gather together.

B. The kitchen, where you like to help out.

C. Anywhere that there is room to twirl!

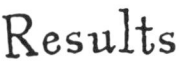

Results

Mostly As

You are a brilliant observer, so your favourite part
will be watching all the fun dance moves!

Mostly Bs

You are very interested in food, so sitting down to have
something to eat will be your highlight! There can be
all sorts of different food at a party, and of course there
will be lots of cake for pudding!

Mostly Cs

You love dancing, so the dancefloor is where
you will have the most fun! You can listen to the
music and dance the night away!

ISADORA · MOON

For more activities
and information about the books,
visit Isadora Moon on Oxford Owl

home.oxfordowl.co.uk/
bookshop/isadora-moon/

For exciting animated Isadora Moon content,
go to @IsadoraMoon on Instagram

To visit Harriet Muncaster's website, visit
harrietmuncaster.co.uk

Harriet Muncaster

Harriet Muncaster, that's me! I'm the
author and illustrator of Isadora Moon.
Yes really! I love anything teeny tiny,
anything starry, and everything glittery.

Love Isadora Moon?
Why not try these too...

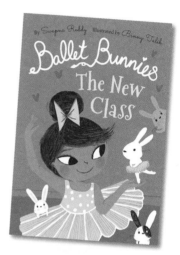